# Make It Egyptian

Pamela Rushby



## Contents


Ancient Egyptians 2

Make an Egyptian Bracelet 4

Make an Egyptian Necklace 8

Make an Egyptian Headdress 12

Fashion Show! 16

# Ancient Egyptians

The ancient Egyptians were a group of people that lived thousands of years ago. They made many amazing things, such as pyramids and temples.

Ancient Egyptians lived in the place we now call Egypt.

Great Pyramid of Giza

The ancient Egyptians also made lots of beautiful jewellery. Jewellery was worn on the neck, wrists, ankles, head and ears.

a necklace

a bracelet

a headdress

# Make an Egyptian Bracelet

Ancient Egyptians liked to wear bracelets on their wrists. The bracelets often had shapes or pictures on them.

- a drawing of a bracelet
- coloured pencils
- hole puncher
- scissors
- two pieces of string – about 15 centimetres long

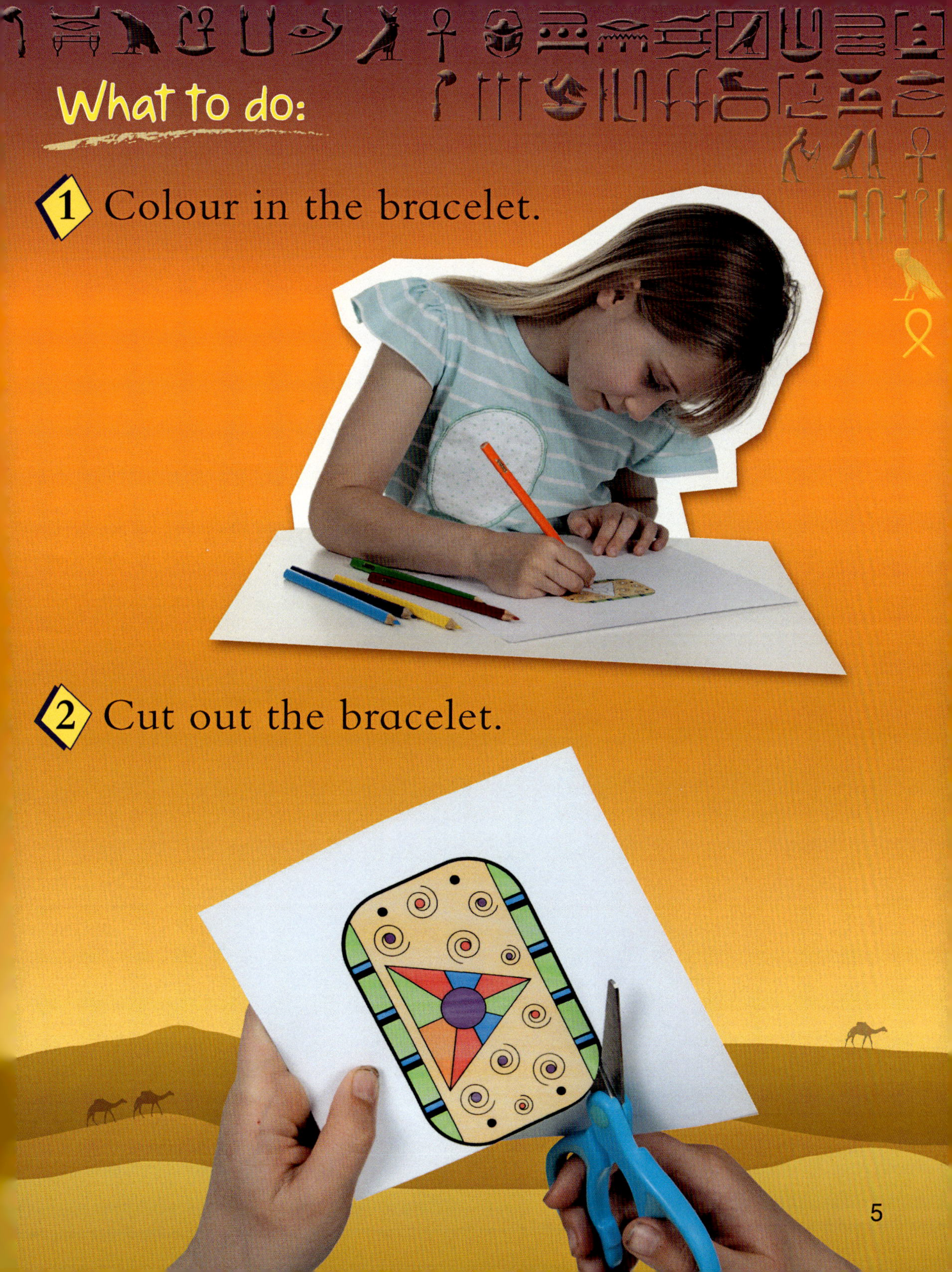

## What to do:

1. Colour in the bracelet.

2. Cut out the bracelet.

3 Punch two holes at both ends of the bracelet.

4 Wrap the bracelet around your wrist.

5 Ask an adult to thread the string into the holes on one end. Do the same at the other end, then tie the string together.

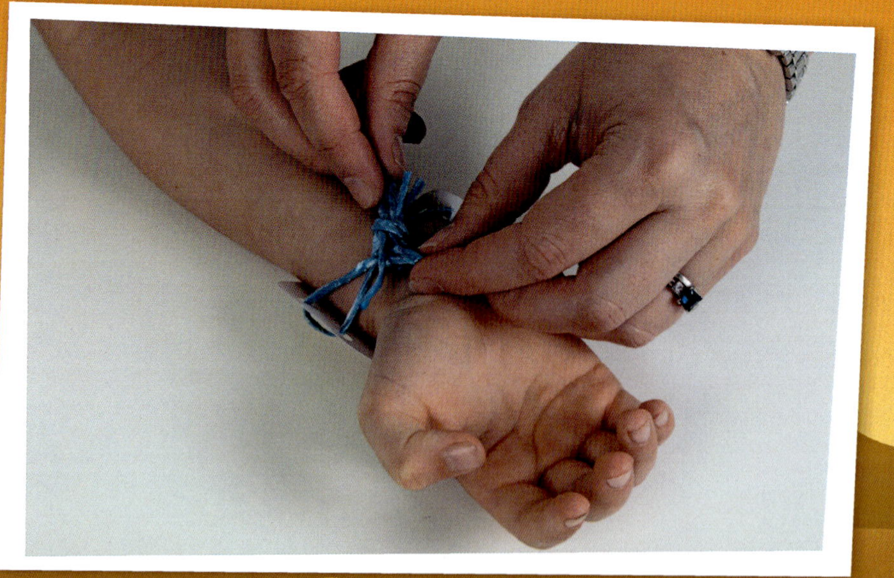

Now you have an Egyptian bracelet!

# Make an Egyptian Necklace

Ancient Egyptians liked to wear necklaces. The necklaces looked like collars. They were made of gold and beads.

## What you need:

- a drawing of a necklace
- coloured pencils
- hole puncher
- glue
- scissors
- string – about 10 centimetres long

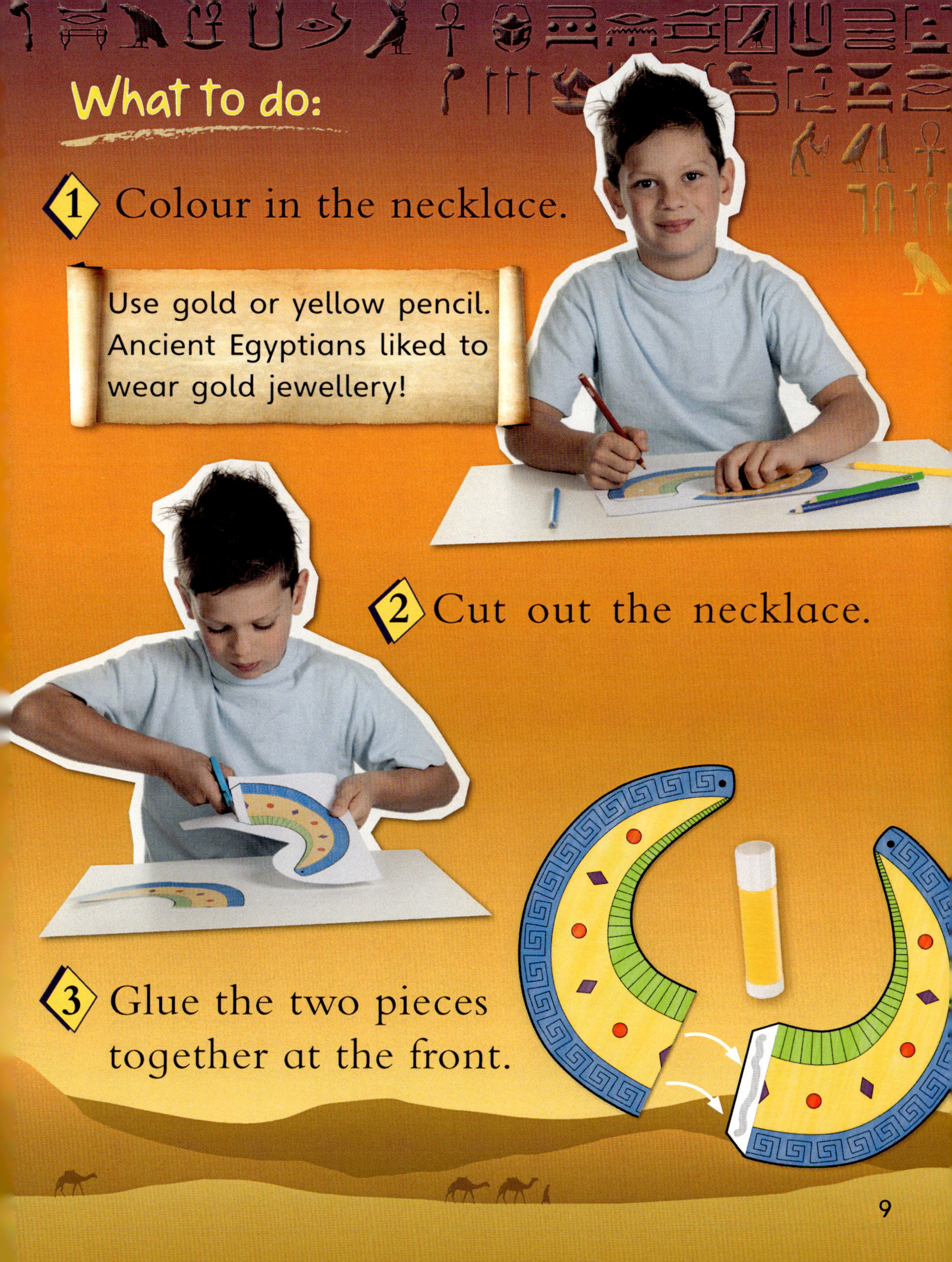

## What to do:

1. Colour in the necklace.

Use gold or yellow pencil. Ancient Egyptians liked to wear gold jewellery!

2. Cut out the necklace.

3. Glue the two pieces together at the front.

4 Punch a hole at both ends.

5 Place the necklace around your neck.

6 Ask an adult to thread the string into each hole and tie the string together.

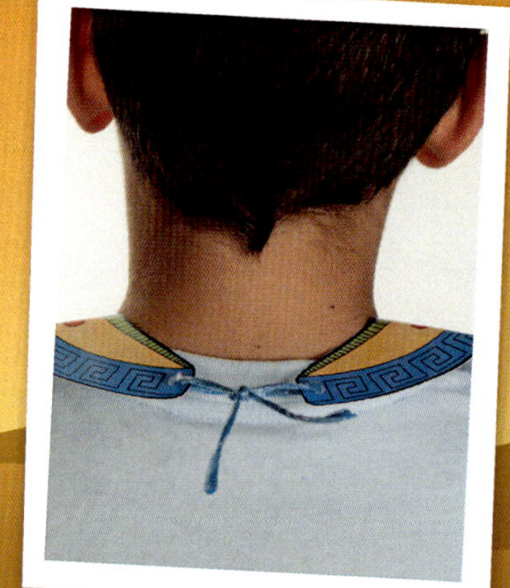

Now you have an Egyptian necklace!

# Make an Egyptian Headdress

Some of the powerful people in ancient Egypt liked to wear headdresses. A headdress is jewellery that is worn on top of the head.

## What you need:

- a drawing of a headdress
- coloured pencils 
- scissors 
- sticky tape 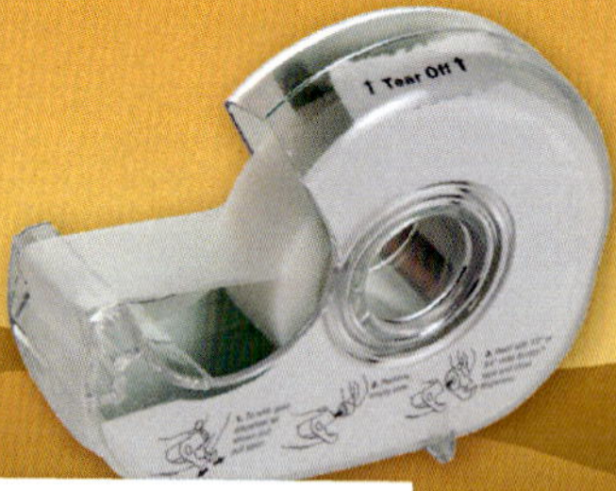
- glue

## What to do:

1. Colour in the headdress.

2. Cut the headdress into three pieces.

two rectangles

the front of the headdress

3. Glue a rectangle to each end of the front piece.

4. Wrap the headdress around your head to check its length. If it is too long, cut off the ends.

Ask an adult to help you.

5. Tape the ends together with sticky tape.

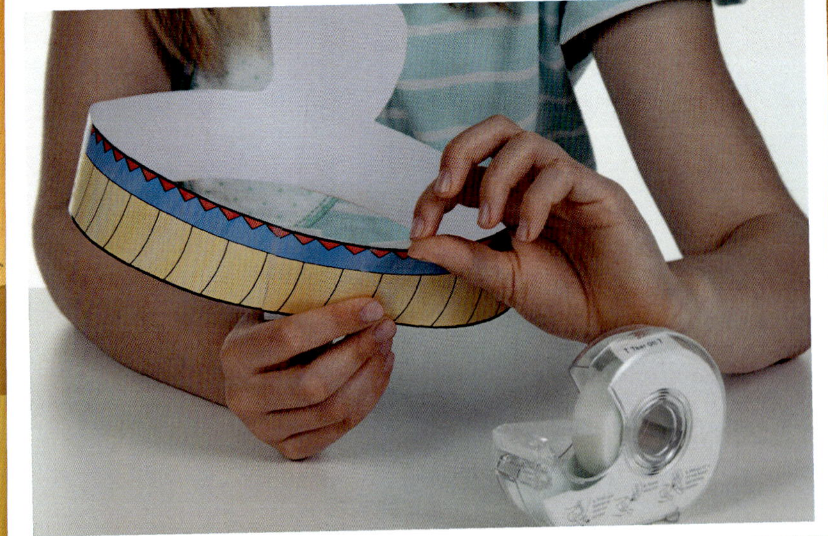

Now you have an Egyptian headdress!

# Fashion Show!

Now that you have made your very own ancient Egyptian jewellery, it is time to show it off! Put on a fashion show for your friends.

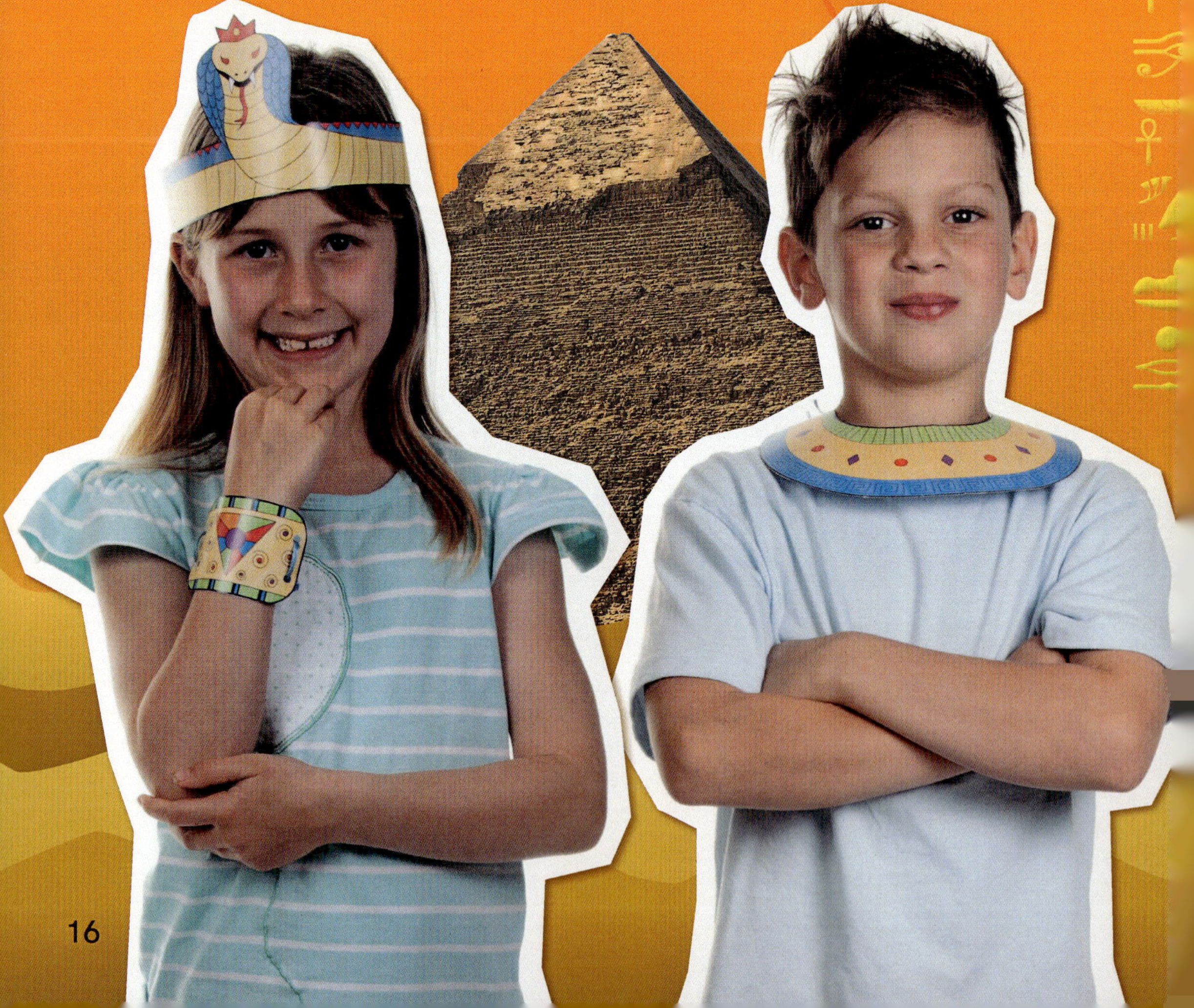